On the shelf of memory

Gopal Patra

ISBN 978-93-5610-277-4

Published in India 2022 by Pencil

A brand of
One Point Six Technologies Pvt. Ltd.
123, Building J2, Shram Seva Premises,
Wadala Truck Terminal, Wadala (E)
Mumbai 400037, Maharashtra, INDIA
E connect@thepencilapp.com
W www.thepencilapp.com

Author biography

Gopal Patra: -

The life of a poet-storyteller is an invincible soldier who fought in battle - whose tool is fearlessness and honesty ... Search Google for details and type in Bengali or English letters.

 If you search "Gopal Patra" you will get all the information!

CONTENTS

On the shelf of memory

On the shelf of memory
Gopal Patra

Dedication:- allteenagers

"Ontheshelfofmemory"

(The story of the first love)

We'veall been through adolescence ... In this adolescence, men and women have all fallen in love in one way or another -
And failed

So do not hesitate to say
Adolescents who fail in 100% love!

At this age, the petals of love buds begin to match come a little closer to each other. A little gossip, a little touching a kiss if too much, so far so good-

Then.

Misunderstandings among themselves or
This love is destroyed in the bud to gain establishment in
life ...

This love or affection in most cases
Doesn't get fullness!

But, in the abyss of the mind, the image of that first
beloved person or person remains ... sometimes it is
scattered - or dormant forever.

Such a pair Sumita and Piyush - their identity from class
seven!

What is the current situation of the two today? Although
their way of life is twisted in two directions
- Still don't feel so much tension between the two -
behind the scenes.

This is a sweet love story "on the shelf of memory"
   Now if the readers are entertained, my work will be
successful!

Gopal Patra: -
The life of a poet-storyteller is an invincible soldier who
fought in battle - whose tool is fearlessness and honesty ...
Search Google for details and type in Bengali or English
letters.
If you search "Gopal Patra" you will get all the
information!

ChapterOne: -

Sumita'seyes suddenly got stuck on Facebook ... on a profile on the ad friend list!

Click on the profile as usual. Sumita is swaying in the light and darkness .. Is this Piyush?
Through self-written poems given to her on her birthday .. Her identity from Class Seven!

But looking at the profile picture, he can't understand ... or why? He is not talking nowadays. - Memories of 25-30 years ago ...

But in a moment the gloom breaks; Just read the message written on the profile ...
"I wanted to swim across the sea.
I wanted to fly in the sky like a balloon ...
I wanted to jump and touch the moon in the sky!

But you didn't ...

I do not know if you will believe? Efforts are still on .. Swimming - Flying in the sky - Jumping to the moon! "

Is this message written for him? Don't be surprised if ... Searching the profile at the speed of the storm, Samita never ends ...

The more you read, the more you are fascinated ... Nakshi kantha of love arranged in layers - the triumph of life - what it takes - poetry - novels - short stories - how much more ...

He eagerly searches for Piyush's family background from his profile - but almost nothing matches!

But is Piyush still alone ...?

What she thinks is as illusory as her fantasy - today her own full family - Bhabanipur High School teacher is her husband too - the girl is in class eight -
He set foot in the forties this year-
Piyush and so be it?
And some hair is tangled ...

Crowds of memories are coming in the blink of an eye ..
that first introduction-birthday gift-sharing school tiffin!
Standing on the school porch in Tiffin and talking ... ...
how much more ...

A picture flashed before my eyes in the classroom - 15th Baishakh, the day before the summer holidays - Sumita's birthday! There is nothing to say about the ceremony, bring a cake to the school tiffin and eat and drink among friends!
Talking about being the first girl in the class is inappropriate if you don't do anything on her birthday!
This mini event is funded by everyone's tiffin money ... who knew in advance - they brought a pen or a Cadbury with them!

Everyone who brought it with them gave it to Sumita ...
The cake was cut as usual - Suddenly someone said Piyush, the second boy in the class - Fast
Didn't give anything on First Girl's Birthday?

I still remember the picture of Sumita ...
Hearing this, Piyush's face turned pale
As if thinking, Piyush suddenly took out a notebook from the bag, tore a page out of it and held it towards Sumita!
Fazil students in the class said in unison or love letter?
Piyush immediately protested in a low voice and said why can it be a love letter? I have nothing to give on Sumita's birthday ... so I gave her a poem written by myself!

B: B - Where do I see poetry? The boy named Apurba snatched the paper from Sumita's hand like a chilen and started reading aloud ...

Happy Birthday ... Happy Birthday ...
As after night -
Let's drop the gold!
Your life in seven colors-
Be colorful!

Happy Birthday ... Happy Birthday.
Be happy
I wish this -
Blessings of the elders after you
Let it always rain!

Happy Birthday..Happy Birthday ...
Let this happy day come back every year ...
Happiness, prosperity and love surround you!

Happy Birthday… Happy Birthday ... that moon in the sky is like a star-
Let the letters be life!
May this world remember you forever!

Piyush took this writing to another level on Sumita's birthday ..

The classroom burst into applause that day ... Piyush's face turned red with embarrassment - and Sumita and I really liked this unexpected award.

That first Piyush
Get acquainted (gain, obtain) with present-day techniques that came from Poetry.

ChapterTwo: -

Amonth of school holidays ... Honestly, Piyush has always been in my mind since then and whenever he remembered, he wanted to read his poems quickly!
But is anyone hiding in the secret place of his teenage mind?

Native Jane Ra thinks love in class seven? Not exactly ... What a pull it felt ...

The tension that can't be swept away - or can't be expressed in words ... that feels like a chinchilla in the corner of the mind ...

Sumita arrived at Piyush's house one day during the summer vacation.
Let's meet once in this thought!

Piyush was sitting in the yard and was busy drawing ... Did you see them and tell them? Where did you sit?

You don't have to be busy! You draw, we're sitting right here ...

I mean ...
Mom, look who's here?

It is better to say that it is not a house but a hut. There are two small rooms.
A widow came out of the hut and introduced Piyush.
This is my mother ...
And this Sumita goes to my school together ... Fast Girls ... Very good girl ...

The lady brought a colorful old mat and asked me to sit down and gave me some water.
And for a while I was surprised to see Piyush's drawings!

In between the words Piyush's mother said don't look at him sometimes
Give me a penny to eat tiffin ...
He doesn't buy tiffin, he buys paintbrushes - he draws pictures ... he has been holding the picture since this morning, he didn't want to eat at noon - he said only eat and drink after finishing the picture! After saying a lot, he sat down to draw again after eating two!

Art paper size is a watercolor painting ...

A huge black crest blossoms red and a few huts below it - The ducks are roaming in the big pond or the lake.

Sumita looks at the picture in amazement and sometimes at the creative man too ... in a vague voice she says beautiful!

Sumita felt like a lotus flower that day ... Talent grew in poverty ...

Piyush was first in Class Six last year when his father died a few days before the exam, leaving him second only to number three ...

Sumita's mind was filled with self-loathing looking at Piyush .. it would have been better if she had been second instead of first!

Impressions of poverty all around are clearly torn mats - torn genji - dirty pants yet always a smile on the face ... there is no shame or effort to cover poverty!

Is this how I understand the happiness of creation?

He himself is the proof that this happiness cannot be found by living in a palace building.

After finishing the picture, Piyush suddenly asked with a smile on his face, how was the picture?

Sumita and his girlfriend both said in unison, very beautiful, very good!

Floating in unprecedented joy, he discovered himself in a new equation.

When he gets any success by himself, he gets excited and pushes his chest - but he also knows anew today that the joy that overwhelms the success of someone else ...

Some such incidents attracted Sumita to Piyush ..

This vision was not Maya or Karuna- how he felt a pull from inside his chest ..

There was little talk in the middle of their class ..

Taking the opportunity, one day he confessed his self-pity to Piyush -

Honestly, if I had known that I would be first for more than three, you would be second, then I would not be first at all!

Sir Rao knew your father had died a few days ago ... then I would have been happier if I had made you fast! But tell me what else to do - but believe me I do not feel good at all!

Piyush smiled softly and said what is your fault? Besides, I learned something I didn't understand in the first second - that's the big thing in getting into a new class!

No matter how many times you ... write poetry, draw such beautiful pictures and my qualification is more than three ...

It doesn't matter if you admit to me that this is what I got a lot!

I was the first to see a talented boy like you. Tell me if you need any help.

I will say ...

During the school tiffin hour, when all the students were busy making tiffin - hoi hullo - Piyush would read a book in class or stand alone on the verandah!

Sumita became a supporter and asked him to share the tiffin once or twice but to no avail ...

Ray is not hungry - because I ate rice in the morning ..

After that, Sumita did not insist - what is the benefit of stabbing self-esteem?

ChapterThree: -

Thenclass eight.
One day Piyush was standing on the verandah and watching what was happening at the bottom of the stairs! Suddenly Sumita sat down and asked, "What are you looking at?"

What a beautiful flower ...

Sumita was shocked and asked, "Where are the flowers?"

Piyush raises his hand and points to the corner of the stairs ...

Sumita notices a small grassy flower tree in a pile of rubbish at the corner of the stairs - filled with very small colorless flowers!

No matter how many times the other students or he himself has been trampled ... no one noticed but Piyush was happy to notice that this is his essence.

Do you notice such a small thing - Ananda Paas?

Yeah Al that sounds pretty crap to me, Looks like Indus aint for me either.

I can't think so much Ray - my solid head - just busy studying ...

Looking at these flowers today, I discovered another thing ..

What is that again?

I don't mean you don't write under your own name ... Write a poem under a pseudonym - I got that pseudonym ...

Do you hear pseudonyms?

Colorless flowers ...

What's not to like about me? Don't look
The pile of jungle has grown into disrespectful negligence! Flowers but flowers have no dignity ... very small and colorless ... so everyone is accustomed to walking in groups without looking - right?

No, I couldn't answer that day - Piyush said these words with a very sad face ... I don't know how much secret pain he had in his mind ...

He is really very poor - his father died a few days ago!
What will he do? How long can you keep all the talent with education? All these thoughts have made Sumita restless for the last few days ...

How many small memories like this are frozen in the
chest ..
That's how a year goes by - Class Nine.

What the school authorities think is that the school
section has been divided evenly
On the basis of numbers i.e. 1-3-5 section A and 2-4-6
section B!

So Piyush and Sumita's classrooms are different according
to the rules - so the range of visits is reduced -

But the exchange of notes continues ...

The day of Saraswati Pujo comes to an end -
And class nine means Saraswati Pujo is in their possession
...

The children of the two sections have shared the
responsibility of work! Sumita insisted on Piyush but did
not agree ...

You answer Piyush indifferently
I do not like it!

Sumita doesn't know why she doesn't like it .. Dad died
during Saraswati Puja! Besides, at that time they have
farming work, which means breaking the paddy weeds ...
That's why no one comes to school pujo in any year - no
homage is given to Piyush ...

This pujo daulake children get a little discount to study -
class nine is one of them ...

It is their responsibility to give invitations to the local school in groups - to bring the marketed idols of Pujo - to decorate the mandapa!

Sumita was in that group and was spending the day in Hai Hai Rai Rai
I don't know ... he may be busy farming! Sumita's mind was racing again and again ..

Well, will you come to pay homage?
Who knows ... Sumita's mind was getting overwhelmed by such thoughts again and again ...

The day of waiting is over ... The day of Saraswati Pujo ... Sumita still remembers that day very much ... Nice to look at ...

Since she is the first girl in the class, her demand in school is very high.
But what will happen if - the same tune of separation jingles the bean of the mind.
Will he come?

Cloudy sky As soon as we reached the school, it started raining heavily ...
Sumita suddenly catches her eye on the school verandah ... not Piyush - alone on the verandah? Who are you waiting for?
Yes, that? Today does not look a little different!

A few steps down the stairs in one fell swoop - Sumita says as she approaches Piyush.
Are you looking at Hadaram like that? Hold my hand, I can't see ...

Yeah Al that sounds pretty crap to me, Looks like Al that sounds pretty crap to me, Looks like Al that sounds pretty crap to me, Looks like Al that sounds pretty crap to me.

At that first touch, heart, mind, soul and body trembled like butterfly wings.

For a moment, though, both of them might have thought that this hand would not be released in life!

So Piyush immediately took out a note size paper and wrote a few words ...

"If you put your hand in this way .. then I will destroy everything ..

If you are next
I will swim across the sea!

If you are close
I will fly in the sky like a lantern ...

If you want, I will jump the moon in the sky! "

Even today, the words written on the messenger on Piyush's Facebook profile ...
Just added ... "You didn't talk"

On the day of Saraswati Pujo, a little conversation in the pouring rain on the school verandah - some gossip and some thoughts on note-sized paper. Sumita liked this piece very much!
On the same day that the love buds of the teenage mind were predicted to blossom ...

At that time, it was not like now that one would walk around the local area holding hands .. The little gossip about giving a wreath together is limited to this ... Both of them had to endure a lot of comments for this ...

Sumita's girlfriend Madhabi shouted and said what is Kiri standing on the verandah?
Pushing Madhuri gently, Suparna said- What will happen to Fast Girls and Second Boy? Exchanging mind notes .... exam preparation- then everyone was laughing ho-ho-!

Sumita is a little embarrassed ... she replied that it is not raining so I stood up - you don't come here either ...

Chapterfour: -

Sumitacouldn't sleep all night that day.
What is the arrival of the south wind in the garden today?

Wouldn't a gentle south wind turn life into a storm one day? This is a little worried about Piyush's emotions ...

Shortly after the final exam, Sumita plunged into her studies without much thought - at that time all the final exams of the school were held in the middle of the month of Falgun and it was almost during Holi or Dolayatra ...
So the color game was far away - I would not leave the house - I would draw pictures in my mind-
Playing Holi with Piyush -

I used to imagine his painted face in the gap of study ...
At that time, there was no Android mobile in the house that would take pictures and send them to each other!

The test is over ... As usual the result is out - Piyush got the third place this time even though the number difference is only five ...
Did Piyush do this on purpose? To sit with him in the same classroom .. but how?

He would have been happier if Piyush had taken the first place ...!

Kiri is the third?
Piyush smiled and said - it is good - I can sit in the same room with you - I mean 1 - 3 odd numbers, that means in section ...

But I wish you were the first -
Is that your number 601 my 594-
Number is simple- don't you know?

But you know how many ups and downs of life depend on number one?

You don't have to think about these thoughts for me! I can't study math ... sorry ...
No, Sumita didn't talk any more that day.

So far so good ...

He himself gave up all the tension and all the love and compassion and settled the account of life in Karaya-Ganda! Why does he have to shake hands with someone today for a little love ... to shake hands for a little fly ...

These days, all these questions are eating away at him - making him bloody day and night ...

Lately, Piyush has made a name for himself by writing poems.

The poem he wrote in the school magazine has spread in the school and the name for being the best - some masters have become a kind of subjugator and take the book of poets from Piyush and with encouragement - congratulations and give occasionally ...

After reading a beautiful love poem in Little Magazine, Samita spontaneously asked Piyush one day -

Well, Piyush, every poet has a human being... whom the poet writes poetry imagining - who is that human being of yours? I know that!
That day Piyush could only say to make her happy - who are you again ... but he didn't say that that day!

Piyush smiled softly and said you are not ... but there is one - I will tell you later ...
Silence for a while, both of you ...

Well, if I imagine you as a human being, then do you have any objection?

Why object? I will consider myself blessed - I will feel lucky! Sumita said the words full of emotion that day!

Piyush was smiling at Titiksha's smile - he said I can bear it.

Of course I can ... why he said that that day - I couldn't catch it ... I got it later -

I did not realize the difference between emotion and reality. Kalpana - Who knew that the real confusion was confusing?

Whatever it is, our friendship is growing a little bit day by day.

Suddenly one day Piyush handed me a note of two or three pages and said read it .. I gladly accepted it!

I was eager to come home ...
This is not a love letter. He said that he was lagging behind in his studies due to his writing and drawing ... I should extend a helping hand to him in reading and listening ...

I am very excited to read this article - the next day I will tell Piyush ... you asked me for help - if I can help a boy like you ... then it will not help me - "will be served" you can rest assured - always me I'll get you ...

That's what I want - remember that but - don't get me wrong? Piyush said ...

Then

One day I told Piyush to keep my promise -

You don't have a private tutor. Come to our house. Sir, if you tell him about your condition, he will take some less money. And my grandfather means my brother-in-law's son, Sajal, teaches English to him, or two days a week, for free!

After thinking for a while, Piyush agreed!

Nagen Sir used to teach regularly at our house at 6 in the morning ... I also try my best to help Piyush as much as possible! It doesn't hurt ...

In this way, the day began to pass in the process of exchanging small mind notes, gradually ...

I have been noticing for some time now that Piyush has become somewhat dependent on me! Of course, it is not the fault of the poor. My behavior is my love.

And who knew that this dependency would one day lead to conflict?

Whatever it is, both of them have done well in the pre-test!

ChapterFive: -

RakhiBandhan Utsav - As is the case at school, donations are made for sweets.
The students in the class can take Rakhi among themselves ...

But Piyush suddenly said- what happens in our class if we celebrate a public Rakhi Bandhan festival ..?

I asked in amazement, what is the meaning of universal rakhi bond? How do you want to observe?

Doesn't it mean that every student in the class will be given rakhi? There will be some sweets ...

That's a lot of money ...
Nice to see that many will not agree to raise money!

No need to raise money ...

I said a little annoyed, then the ghost will come and pay?

Why ghosts? I'll pay ...

You mean, like, saltines and their ilk, eh? Chisa recovered the money or not?
You don't have to worry so much, tell me if you agree?

If you can afford it - do it ... I can't give up when you want to! I said the words a little angrily ...

Get angry, it will be a social work, know ...

Didn't say anything that day - but I thought to myself - did such a social worker come? That himself comes to school with a rat-cut shirt, an old pants-torn bag! Whether he will do social work!

I immediately thought the opposite, how many really like him? How many people have big minds like him? I got a friend like him ... I was so happy to think of that!
Wondering where to get the money?

During the day, Rakhi Bandhan was celebrated in the school with pomp and circumstance.

It was my responsibility to give sweets at the request of Piyush!

Many of us kept our hands separate to keep the two of us apart ...

It seems that this time our first class girl Sumita will wear Piyush's Rakhi ...

The classroom was filled with applause.

I tied a rakhi brought by Piyush and tied it in his hand .. I gave him a sweet in my own hand and Piyush fed me a sweet too!

Clap your hands again ...

I saw such a program for the first time. I read in that book. In 1905, Rabindranath Tagore started to abolish the Partition of Bengal.

I liked it very much, but there were some things in my chest - especially where he got so much money?

So at the end of the program, I told Piyush that I would walk home with you today.

Is that right? He said ...

Walking side by side after school holidays -

After being silent for a while, he said, tell me what to say? I pressed the ball first, really tell me, where did I get all this money?

Surely not stolen?

No, I'm not saying that - I don't know ... I don't have the right to know where I got all this money from.

Of course there is ...

Dad, don't say that without Vanita ...

I applied for a local V, D, O, where if you have 80% marks, you can get a scholarship of two thousand rupees every year in Nine and Train classes ... I got that money last week ...

I used that money to celebrate Rakhi Bandhan at my village home and at school!

When did you do it at home?

7am to 10pm ...

Was it sweet with Rakhi there?

No, I couldn't make sweets there because there must be hundreds of children together ... I put them there and there were two lollipops!

What did the man of the house, your mother, know about money?

Did you know ...

Then did not tie?

No ... because I save Tiffin's money and celebrate Rakhi Bandhan every year at my village home!

After all the self-loathing is gone, a new sun of the mind rises - a glimpse is painted ...

Another foolish day
I asked Rakhi, did you not think of anything to stop it?

Why - what do you think?

I mean ... I mean ... the exchange of Rakhi between Arki siblings ... what do you mean ...

Piyush said with a big smile, "I understand you ..."
No- no, why should I think of all that?
You are my best friend ... I will be your girlfriend forever
.....

Chaptersix:-

Piyush, I could not keep your word ... I could not keep the dignity of your faith ... I have betrayed you - so even today I get bloody wounds every moment - in secluded solitude ....

At the end of the Rakhi bond at school, Piyush made a short speech which was summarized as follows ....

We were all friends in class, we are friends - but today the friendship is stronger through Rakhi Bandhan - it is stronger ...
In the next few months we will face the biggest test of our lives so that everyone can do well in this test so today we are committed - we can extend a helping hand to each

other!
And for this collaboration we need to arrange a class among ourselves after the school holidays ...
In that class, the one who is the most proficient among us will discuss how to get higher marks in that subject!

Seres take different classes but many of us can't speak our minds which means our advantages and disadvantages -
Since it will not be among the friends! And if you open your mind, the matter will be clear! So classes will start from next Monday for those who are willing to join - how can we meet again after the Monday break ...

How many new thoughts would arise in his white mind - and he would try hard to give it a face ...

But not all eyes are the same.
Hemant Da Head, a fourth class employee of the school, listens to the students as soon as the class starts after the school holidays. ...

So one day later the headmaster called some of us including Piyush ...

Piyush Head Sir as much as possible
Trying to explain - we give him white ...

After listening to us, Sir said, "Okay, you keep going ... but if we keep watch, I will stop!"

We agreed and left Sir's room ... Some of the students were cut off due to misunderstanding between us.
Although I did not want to stay, I could not leave looking at Piyush's face!

Within a few days, the head sir suddenly came to our class শুনে he heard us talking and praised us and gave us permission to continue the class!

But our selfishness came to an end and within a few days the class was closed, meaning that those who were skilled in the subject would think of their own interests - they did not agree to help later!

On the day of the decision to break the class, on the way back to school, I told Piyush that I was not sorry ... You wanted the best for everyone, but I don't want everyone to be the best ... I didn't want that either!
What can be done? If you continue to study well, you will no longer have to worry about others!

ChapterSeven: -

Piyushwas feeling very depressed that day - he looked very bad but what can be done? The storm that blows over the people ...

In the midst of regular study, the mind is tucked away, this is how time passes for a while ...

Competing with Piyush, I have become a bit careless - the loss of education is lately ...

Because I can't understand exactly how Piyush always remembers a tight feeling as if my world revolves around

him!
 You can't go on like this - you can't let go - the big test of life ahead - must be established at any cost!
 Besides, I have felt together with Piyush for a few years - the difference between his mind and mine is sky-deep!

 But is it his mercy? Not love? Sumita can't do self-analysis - but she has to wear that!

 Lately, thinking like this, Sumita avoids Piyush a bit!

 Piyush feels this avoidance in his mind but does not say anything in his mouth!
 Coming to tuition, Piyush notices the feeling of death - the mind is overwhelmed but he also remains silent ...

 After a while -
 Sumita's English notebook was with Piyush one day and he returned the notebook and said - if there is anything written in it, read it ... Sumita doesn't answer!

 Anamne opened the notebook once and saw many written poems.

 At the end of reading, I am lying down at night reading the writings - the writings can be called poems and also the letters can be said.

 At that time my room mate means my sister Manisha is present and you are still studying? I see what you are reading? He snatched the book ..

 I'm shocked ... of course ...

After a while Didi said - what have you done? Your future will eat the whole thing ... The boy who came to the tuition in the morning in a half-dirty dress with a broken bicycle - Wait, Dad - I'm telling Mom!

I hold her hand and foot in hapless eyes and tell her to stop reading from tomorrow - and tell her not to have any relationship with me.
I promised you - I will not have any more relationship!
Please do not tell parents!

You promised but- Didi said!

I said yes ....

Didn't sleep all night that day - I waited for Piyush to come to tuition in the morning with irritated eyes!
If necessary, I will threaten Piyush along with my sister ... She will behave like this- never again! And from today e does not have any relationship with him!

No, Piyush didn't come to tuition that day ...
Going to school for two periods
As soon as the bell rang, Piyush was taken by three or four friends to the verandah of Dakmam School -

I showed the book in front of everyone and asked Piyush - have you become a great poet?
What are you writing?
What do you think of yourself?
Did you buy the head because it extended the hand of friendship so much? I do not have any respect? This is your writing .. keep it with you ... never bother me with any

writing in the future! Don't have any relationship with me from today - don't even try to talk - I said this!

Didn't say anything in favor of Piyush -
Just when I left - then his white pale face - pleaded - talk to me alone for five minutes about this - see if everything will be fine ...

Five minutes, why one minute and he does not want to talk to you!

Fifteen or twenty days is a long way from tuition - Piyush is not even coming to school ...

I didn't feel any pain ... I didn't eat well for three days - I couldn't sleep!
I don't keep calm, I keep cool ...
At that time it was not like now, now I see many girls running away from home in class nine are getting married! But that time was different, we were afraid of the people of the house like yam!

In which story did I read in the novel The Easy Way to Kill People?
Love someone (act) when he is dependent on you - move away from him - then he will die on his own!

Am I a murderer then? Didn't I use that tie with Piyush?

Didn't I destroy his talents with Piyush in the shoot? This thought made me bloody-shocked ...

Piyush came to school for the first time today, almost a month after the test ...
I can't look at him with a slender body - for a man a man

breaks down like this .. his poverty has become clear - today he really looks very poor ...

In the midst of hundreds of poverty, he always had a soft smile on his face - the impression of poverty was on his clothes - not on his face!

A popular song of that time was sung by Kumar Shanu,
Is that really so?

Ma'am - Sirera wants to know why Piyush hasn't come to school for so long - Piyush is trying his best - to say ... but suddenly Hemant Da, a fourth class employee, said. If Ila Ma'am-Absent in English is not submitted in writing, she will not be allowed to sit for the test ...

Piyush took the test on time but the result was not good. He could not get the name of the fast list.

In front of me, many people have jokingly said - these new thoughts - Rakhi Bandhan - to take classes with students! The result of writing poetry!

Piyush has endured all the jokes ... did not protest so much!

Then school three months off -
As per the results of the board's secondary examination, Piyush did not get first division for some numbers.

I got letters in four subjects - I got the first place in the school - what a great success - I'm not a good girl?

Chaptereight: -

    Ourschool is limited to secondary so I was forced to enroll in the first year of Amata Pitamber - and I heard that Piyush was admitted to N-D College!

One day I met him in Debal Sir's English class - Piyush Debal Sir will have tuition I heard before from one of his friends! Piyush had come one day but seeing me, he probably never came again!

Then Piyush did not find out and I came to H- from engrossed in studies..with good result I went to study in UP with honors in geography ...
Baruipur school teacher came back from there!

Then after a couple of years
Arnab K is a teacher of that school
I got married with a kind of love ...

Now both of us ... Master - Masterni - Office - The house is under the same roof ... Husband and wife, when you have time and opportunity, teach each other well! The only girl in class eight stays in the hostel ....

Last year I bought 20 lakh flats near the school in installments - there are also new four wheels a ...

But when I went to show other countries on the map of the world, I forgot my own country!

While studying the origin of the Himalayas, I can smell a great smell ...

What causes a volcanic eruption?
By the way, I am carrying a burning volcano in my chest!

But Piyush, wherever you are, as you think - the proof that you are living the impossible is his Facebook profile ...

Today I do not know how much weight your body or the world? But you still fly in your mind ... like a bird - like a balloon! The moon still shakes your hand -
You still giggle at the flower ...

People do not die in hundreds of repercussions ... Life swims in the sea alone ... From today I also started swimming upstream of you - if two people meet in the middle of the sea ... then maybe we will be rescued together ....
Or I will be drowned forever in the abyss ....